Text and illustrations copyright © Alan Marks 1998

First published in Great Britain in 1998
by Macdonald Young Books
an imprint of Wayland Publishers Ltd
61 Western Road
Hove
East Sussex
BN3 1JD

Find Macdonald Young Books on the internet at
http://www.myb.co.uk

The right of Alan Marks to be identified as the author
and illustrator of this Work has been asserted by him in
accordance with the Copyright, Designs and Patents Act 1988.

Designed and Typeset by Backup Creative Services, Dorset DT10 1DB
Printed and bound in Belgium by Proost International Book Production

British Library Cataloguing in Publication Data available

ISBN: 0 7500 2501 8

ALAN MARKS

The
Beachcomber

MACDONALD YOUNG BOOKS

Chapter One

On a high-tide one spring morning, a strange
young boy came to the beach. Some said he
came in the old beachcomber's boat, others
that he just walked out of the sea. He took
to living in the old hut on the shingle.
No one knew where he had come from.
And, since he had no mother or father,
the local people said that it seemed the sea
must be looking after him.

Before the boy came, Daniel, the old beachcomber, had lived in the hut on the shingle. For as long as anyone could remember, the old man had made a living by what he'd found along the shoreline. Like the boy, the sea gave him what he needed.

The old beachcomber drove a hard bargain when he found fishing nets washed up on the beach and sold them back to the fishermen. Yet they always trusted his knowledge of the weather and wouldn't put to sea against his advice.

He would also tell them where the herring could be found.

How did he know such things? No one knew for sure but there were some that said the waves told him.

Then one day the old beachcomber disappeared without trace.

Chapter Two

Alice remembered Daniel the beachcomber. She had grown fond of the old man and missed him when he went away. Now she often saw the young boy walking the tide-line just as the old beachcomber had done. But she had not been brave enough to speak to the boy.

Then one day, after she had watched her father's boat sail from sight, Alice met the boy sitting by a breakwater watching the clouds.

"The wind is getting up," said the boy. "It'll bring the fish inshore and the boats will follow; your father will be home for tea."

Alice looked hard at the boy. He was a little older than her but surely not old enough to know the ways of the sea.

"How do you know that?" she asked, sitting down out of the breeze. "You sound like the old beachcomber."

"Now, he did know a thing or two," said the boy, turning to look at Alice. "He knew the sea and could read the weather like a page in a book."

How this strange boy knew the beachcomber was a mystery but, sensing that he had a story to tell, Alice sat back against the breakwater and let the boy continue...

… Once, after a mighty storm, the beachcomber found a great treasure lying amidst the shells and driftwood. The beauty of it made him weep and its value was beyond anything you could imagine. Whether it was a giant pearl or a fabulous carved sea-horse or Neptune's gold the old man would not say. You might think that after a lifetime of searching the pebbles the old man would take this great prize as his due. But he never hoped to keep it for himself, only to keep it safe. He knew where things belonged.

The old man never said a word about what he had found. But his silence must have sounded like a fog-horn, because it became known in far corners that 'The Beachkeeper' held something very precious.

One night, not long after finding the treasure, the beachcomber was dozing by the fire in his hut. Above the cracking and hissing of the driftwood came a roaring sound like wind in the chimney. A light brighter than the fire flooded the hut and the beach beyond.

The old man ran outside. He expected
to see flares from a ship in danger. But
the light had not come from the sea!

On the road above the beach a gigantic
dragon stood, burning the night with its
breath. The creature was so huge that its
eyes might have been stars.

14

15

When the old man ran from his hut it lurched towards him, sending another torch of flame across the beach. The old beachcomber ran into the sea and stood waist deep in water to face the creature.

'Beachkeeper!' roared the dragon. 'You have something for me. I'll take it now.'

The beachcomber was no fool. He knew where things belonged.

'You can singe my beard,' he called back, 'but I have nothing for you. Fire would melt the treasure that I hold.'

The beast roared such that there might never be peace again. Its great tail thrashed the shingle to sand. The fire in its breath turned night into day. But for all it raged, it dared not go to the water's edge.

Screaming with anger, the dragon
vanished in a ball of fire as bright as
the sun.

When only the stench of sulphur
remained, the old man walked back to the
beach. In the darkness he could hear the
sea sweeping the shingle on the shoreline.
The old man spoke back to the sea.
'There'll be more of this,' he said.

Chapter Three

Alice glanced uneasily up to the road
above the beach and edged a little closer
to the boy. He looked at her kindly and
went on with the story…

… A day or two on, the beachcomber was walking the tide-line. A great quantity of coal had washed ashore, probably from a steamer in the channel. This was treasure that the old man could keep or sell!

On stooping to gather the coal his eye was drawn again to the road, where a huge chestnut mare stood, snorting and stamping the ground. In a moment, spurred on by its great, red-faced rider, the giant horse came crashing on to the pebbled beach. It stopped short of the tide-line and jangled its bridle defiantly.

'I'll take what's mine, Beachkeeper!'
cried the horseman. Stinking clods of
earth clung to the horseman's hair and
clothes. The old beachcomber stared up
at the monstrous horse. Dead creatures
hung from its bridle: rats, moles, weasels,
squirrels. The jangling was not of brass
but of bones.

'You may take what is yours,' replied the beachcomber, 'but I have nothing that belongs to you. Earth would crush the treasure that I hold.'

The horseman shifted angrily in the saddle and he kicked his spurs hard into the mare's flanks. The mare made as to charge, but would not cross the tide-line. She stamped and snorted furiously.

The horseman raised his whip again and again, beating the animal without mercy. Rearing wildly, the horse threw its rider and trampled him to dust.

In no time there was nothing but compost for the sea holly. The horseman had returned to the earth from where he came.

The musty smell of the earth seemed to calm the great horse. As if released from a spell, she shook her head and bowed gently to the beachcomber. She turned and galloped away, shaking the bones from her bridle as she ran free.

Once again the old beachcomber could hear only the sea whispering on the shingle.

Chapter Four

Again Alice glanced up to the road. "Does this story have a happy ending?" she asked warily.

"In a way this story has no ending," said the boy, "but I think the story is a happy one…"

… The third caller almost fooled the old beachcomber. She came on a warm afternoon. The old man had had a good day. A crate of fish had washed ashore, still fresh, and cork floats that he could exchange with the fishermen.

Turning his back to the sea, he saw a young girl standing a little way from him. Perhaps because she was pretty and looked as light as air, he walked over to her.

'You are keeping something for me,'
she said. She smiled such that the old
beachcomber thought that there could
be no harm in her.

'Perhaps I am,' he replied, thinking
that she could not have crossed the
tide-line if she meant ill.

The old man invited her to walk with him to his hut.

Walk with him she did, matching his every stumbling step. Almost at the door of his hut, the old man became wary.

'Wait here,' he said. 'I'll fetch what's yours.' He moved quickly to the door and stopped before entering.

Greedy for the treasure, the girl could not wait. She followed after the beachcomber but too late to match his stride. The old man realized then that she made no sound on the shingle and her feet had not touched a single pebble.

'Fire would melt and Earth would crush the treasure that I keep,' said the canny old man. 'And what would sink in Water cannot be held by Air. I have seen through you, Air spirit. I have nothing that belongs to you.'

Indeed he could see through her.
As he spoke, the spirit began to dissolve
in the afternoon sunshine. The pretty
young face became that of an ugly
phantom. Its gaping mouth wailed and
screamed in protest.
'You cannot keep it,
Beachkeeper, it will
be the end of you...!'

The sunshine was blackened by cloud.
A tantrum wind hit the beachcomber's hut
like a storm wave hits the side of a ship.

The old man clung to the doorway and
hoped his roof would hold. He'd never
known a fiercer wind. Then, like all
tantrums, this one came to a sobbing,
sniffing end. Once more the sunlight
glinted at the sea's edge.

Chapter Five

As the boy had predicted, a strong wind
now blew from the sea. The clouds moved
towards the beach, turning grey as they
approached. Alice shifted a little against
the breakwater. "Does the sea come for
its treasure now?" she asked eagerly.

"Just as the old beachcomber knew that it would," said the boy, "and he knew that when the sea comes calling it is best to wait indoors..."

... By dusk the waves were rolling on the beach. By the time the old man had closed his shutters and bolted his door, the sea was piling shingle high above the tide-line. Great foaming crests came booming and slapping along the shoreline, somersaulting to the beachcomber's door.

Lying in his bunk, the old man could hear spray from the waves raining against the painted planking of his hut. More than once the sea itself came pounding at the door.

All night the old man slept in fits
and woke in starts to the roar of the sea.
Each time he woke he was surprised still
to be dry in his bunk. Each time he slept
he dreamt of fishing boats pitching on
impossible waves. He heard the calls of
drowning men and the silence of ships
rusting on the sea floor.

In the early morning, the beachcomber woke again and wondered at the silence. The storm had ceased. The gulls had not stirred. He heard then the faint sweeping of the surf on the shingle and knew the sea was calling.

The beachcomber carried the sea's treasure, wrapped in sailcloth, outside on to the beach. The silver light of early dawn can trick the eye, and the old man had reason enough to think that he was still dreaming.

He saw a million glistening figures lining the shore. To each side of the hut the line stretched along the waterfront for as far as he could see. Some figures sat on white horses, others rode in chariots or ghostly boats. Many stood at the sea's edge watching the beachcomber.

There were children and elders and all
ages between among the shimmering
figures. As one moved an arm or turned
its head so the others followed in turn,
sending silver waves along the beach.

The beachcomber spread the sailcloth on the pebbles in front of him and stepped back. The tallest of the figures moved forward, stirring a surge of movement along the line. A surf of figures flooded the sailcloth and the lost treasure was taken among them.

The tallest of them spoke in a distant voice that sounded like the sea whispering along the shingle. Its voice echoed along the line, 'Thank you, Beachkeeper. For returning this treasure you may choose another. The sea has many riches that once belonged to men. What would you choose?'

The beachcomber scratched his head.
The greatest treasure he could think of
was a spar of timber to prop the roof of
his hut; a bottle of rum for winter cheer
or better still a message in a bottle, drifted
across from a distant land.

'If I have riches then I have no living,' was the old man's reply. 'I would have no need to walk the tide-line, no reason to stir from my bunk.' The old man looked down to the shingle. Without hesitating he said, 'I would like another lifetime of looking and the hope of finding something good.'

'If you choose that then you must come with us,' came the echoing voice.

Chapter Six

"The old man left the beach on that strange tide," continued the boy. "His small boat was taken out by the foaming surf of figures. The fishermen and the local people haven't seen him since. His hut stayed empty for a while. The coal and the driftwood piled up on the tide-line and the shingle began to cover the little treasures that the sea leaves behind.

"Then one spring morning on the flood-tide, a bright young boy came to the beach and took to living in the hut where the old beachcomber used to live. The boy knew the sea and could read the weather like a page in a book."

Speechless, Alice looked from the boy to the sea and back again to the boy. "That's the end, or the beginning, of the story," he said. "And here come the fishing boats, following the fish inshore." Alice looked towards the horizon and saw the fishermen coming home.

The boy had moved away along the beach. Alice watched him walking the tide-line, leaning forward into the wind. "What's your name?" she called after him.

"Daniel," returned the boy, "just like the old beachcomber."

Look out for more titles in the Red Storybooks series:

The Thief's Daughter by Alan Marks
One fine morning, Magpie glimpses something glinting on the path.
The moment she picks it up, Magpie knows it's something special:
a tiny gold key. But little does she realise what extraordinary secrets the
mysterious key will unlock... *SATS title*

Thomas and the Tinners   Jill Paton Walsh • Alan Marks
Thomas works in the tin mine where he meets some fairy miners who
cause him a great deal of trouble – but then bring good fortune.
WINNER OF THE SMARTIES PRIZE.

Birdy and the Ghosties   Jill Paton Walsh • Alan Marks
Birdy has second sight, but has no use for her gift until the day the
ghosties arrive...

Matthew and the Sea Singer   Jill Paton Walsh • Alan Marks
Birdy buys an orphan boy for one shilling. The boy, Matthew, has a
wonderful gift: he has a voice like an angel's. But one day Matthew goes
missing. Where could the boy with the beautiful voice have gone?

The Sea Horse   Anthony Masters • James Mayhew
Jamie is swimming in the sea when he gets caught by a strong current
and is in danger of drowning. Suddenly a magnificent white horse appears
and takes him safely to the shore. But then the horse is captured by a
cruel farmer. Can Jamie rescue him?

You can buy all these books from your local bookseller, or they can
be ordered direct from the publisher. For more information about
Storybooks, write to: *The Sales Department, Macdonald Young Books,
61 Western Road, Hove, East Sussex BN3 1JD*